harlem moon
broadway books
new york

a

little

piece

of

sky

To Sister Stacy
Remember that
hope is as endless
as the sky.
Nicole
H/27/03

NICOLE

BAILEY-WILLIAMS

Harlem Moon titles may be purchased for business or
promotional use or for special sales. For information,
please write to: Special Markets Department,
Random House, Inc., 280 Park Avenue, New York,
NY 10017.

PRINTED IN THE UNITED STATES OF AMERICA

The figure in the Harlem Moon logo is inspired by a
graphic design by Aaron Douglas (1899–1979).
HARLEM MOON and its logo depicting a moon and
woman, are trademarks of Broadway Books, a
division of Random House, Inc.

Visit our website at www.harlemmoon.com

DESIGNED BY JENNIFER ANN DADDIO

Library of Congress Cataloging-in-Publication Data
Bailey-Williams, Nicole.
A little piece of sky / Nicole Bailey-Williams.—1st
ed.
p. cm.
1. African American girls—Fiction. 2. Single-parent
families—Fiction. 3. Mothers and
daughters—Fiction. 4. Philadelphia (Pa.)—Fiction.
5. Mothers—Death—Fiction. I. Title.

PS3552.A3748 L58 2002
813'.6—dc21
2001051949

First Edition published 2002.

ISBN 0-7679-1216-0

10 9 8 7 6 5 4 3 2 1

acknowledgments

I thank the Divine Spirit for divine guidance.

There are many people whose nurturing kindness has assisted me in bringing this project to fruition. At the top of the list is my husband, Gregory, who understands my need to make sense of the world with a pen. My parents, Robert and Adrean Bailey, have provided constant encouragement for my writing from the first time that I hunted and pecked on Mom's typewriter from her Cheyney days to Dad's lugging around textbooks for me while I conducted research for my first national publication. My brother, Michael Bailey, has been a wonderful "board" off of which I have bounced ideas. In fact, he was chauffeuring me around when the title first came to me. My grandmothers, Sugar Ellis and Irene Bailey, planted two very different seeds of strength in me, while my grandfathers, Louis Ellis and J. Crafton Stukes, nurtured silent wisdom. All of them are thanked for their contributions to my development. My godparents, Odell "Pat" Patterson and Mary Patterson, have supported my every step with their love, devotion, and guidance.

I have been blessed to have numerous "co-parents" in my life. They have, along with my parents, helped to shape me into my current self by providing real-life stories of triumph and strength. Baxter and Stallworth families, take a bow. You are my heroes.

Outside of my family, many other people have provided much support for me by reading for me or listening as I read. In alphabetical order, they are Sharon Baxter, Van Robinson, Barbara Trainor, and Danielle Williams. Thank you for your extra sets of eyes. My "sister," Darlise Blount, blows inspirational wind in my direction even when we haven't spoken for a while, and for that, she, too, is thanked.

I also thank Kelley Kenner and her family for their support.

Other people whose input has been invaluable along this journey include Dr. Paula Barnes, Colin Channer, Delin Cormeny, Kate Garrick, Patricia Haley, Tamlin Henry, my editor Janet Hill, William July II, Diane McKinney-Whetstone, Karen Quinones Miller, and Omar Tyree. Thank you for your encouragement and advice.

I say thank you to Charlotte Abbott, Lynn Andriani, Johnny J. Butler, William Cox, Sanyu Dillon, Michelle Gibson, Nira Hyman, Adrienne Ingrum, Jimyce Johnston, Dawn Angelique Jones, Mondella Jones, and Max Rodriguez for assisting me in finding a national forum for my writing.

There are a number of people who helped to make the self-published version a success. I thank them in no particular order. Here goes: my Sorors of Delta Sigma Theta Sorority, Inc., my church family at Cedar Park Presbyterian, Dave and Shante Warren and their book club, Felicia Polk, Soror Keena Cravison, Robin Green-Cary of Sibanye Books in Baltimore, Judy Sylvester, Jack Watro,

Linda Watson and the Coalition for 100 Black Women, Myra and the Philadelphia TWIGS, my sisters from the National Association of University Women, Tonya Richardson, The Beta Delta Zeta Chapter of Zeta Phi Beta Sorority, Inc., Phyllis Meekins, Alice Wright of Allie's Jazz Bistro in Philadelphia, Lecia and Shiela at Basic Black Books in Philly, Janifer Wilson at Sisters Uptown Bookstore in New York, Brooke A. McCauley, Bert at Waldenbooks in Renaissance Center in Detroit, Nkenge at Shrine of the Black Madonna Bookstore in Detroit, Marcus Williams at Nubian Bookstore in Morrow, Georgia, Tony Cannida, The Shabazzes of Haneef's Bookstore in Wilmington, Delaware, Erica Green, Dr. Jean Moore of Temple Public Radio (WRTI-Philadelphia) Mind & Soul Bookstore in Trenton, New Jersey, Tom and Gwen Pope, Keith Leaphart, Ms. Betty and Mr. Ligorius of Ligorius Bookstore in Wyncote, Pennsylvania, Doc Cunningham, Bruce at The Know Bookstore in North Carolina, Cousin Angel Ellis, Lorraine Ballard-Morrill of Power 99 FM (WUSL-Philadelphia), Harriet at Waldenbooks in Newark,

Delaware, Cait LaMonica, Vanesse Lloyd-Sgambati, Temi Dada in Orange, New Jersey, Hayden at Robin's Bookstore in Philadelphia, Scott Mitchell of CBC, Onah Weldon and the National Political Congress of Black Women, Ronni Holzendorf, The Philadelphia Metropolitan Area Chapter of the Continentals, Kwame and Stephanie Alexander, Sparkle Book Club in Delaware, Tonya Johnson and the Philadelphia Kappa Silhouettes, Linda Meade and the National Kappa Silhouettes, Graina Noble, Carrie Cole at Dygniti Books in Connecticut, the Bucks and Montgomery County Chapters of Jack and Jill of America, Brett at Positive Vibes in Virginia Beach, Virginia, Sharon Thorn of Cheyney University, Claudette Parrott, the administrators at Paine College in Augusta, Georgia, Sorors from Delta Authors on Tour, Brenda Brisbaine and Sisters with a Purpose Book Club, Marie of Majoco Collection in Plainfield, New Jersey, Dr. Barbara Gadegbeku, Kim Kenefick, Rose Miller and the Bucks County Chapter of The Links, Naima Smith and Maureen Forrest of the Nassau Alumnae Chapter of DST, Monique

Ford, Sally Johnson and The Friday Salon Book Club, Venus and Pamela of Waldenbooks in Maryland, Vanessa Miller, Rob Dixon (WHOV-Hampton, Virginia), Linda Crooks, Soror Vanessa Parker, A. M. Weaver and Art Sanctuary, Amina Gautier, Cozette Ferron and Imhotep Charter Academy, Simba Sonna at Karibu, Malik, Jamellah, and Jair Ellis, Cousin Annette Ellis, Soror Nancy Flowers Wilson, Trust at Nubian Heritage, Harriet Memeger and the Delta Book Club, Al Hunter, and Juanita Brown and the Dear Sisters Book Group.

I also wish to thank everyone who purchased the self-published version of "my baby." Your faith in my writing gave me the extra push.

morning

running

My mother was always running away. I suppose it's only natural because she came from a long line of runners. Her grandmother ran away from Virginia to Connecticut, where she worked as a cleaning woman in a hotel. Her mother, my grandmother, ran away from Connecticut to Philadelphia, where she settled on the southwest side, long before the airport was built. My mother ran away, but not as far as her foremothers had run, for she had too much baggage to carry, and this was no easy task for a solitary woman. She simply got on the trolley one day, and when she looked out the window, she saw a kite the color of water dancing in the sky. She gathered up her things and bustled off the trolley, trying to follow the kite that was free. She walked and she walked and she walked, struggling with her load, chasing the liberated kite, which she never could catch. Eventually, she got tired and sat on a step to catch her breath. That was where she planted herself. There in the section of North Philly teeming with golden, tan, cream, and bronze people. She heard the cadence of their tongue and decided that she loved them, for they, too, were travelers. They, too, felt that they didn't belong in one place, so they packed up their things and ventured to a new place. My mother never could understand why they would leave the place that God had kissed with sun long before the conquistadors came, but she respected their bravery, so there she stayed, waiting for the kite the color of water to remember her and come back.

my birth

Sometimes I wonder if there was any joy at my birth. Did people gather in the waiting room of the hospital anticipating my arrival? Were anxious phone calls made from one relative to the next? Did my mother look into my eyes and think that I could do something special? Did she think that I might be the first black President or the scientist who discovers the cure for some dreaded disease? Did she try to convey her purest, deepest hopes from her heart to mine? Probably not. I tried asking her about it one day, but it must not have been the right time. She had just opened her beer, and it hadn't had enough time to fill in the empty spaces, to blur the hard edges of her reality. So she told me to shut the hell up. And I did.

I know that my dad probably didn't pass out cigars upon hearing the news. He was married, and I was just one more thing to hide from his wife.

I wonder how I can ever be happy if happiness was not at my spring.

my outer self

The skin I'm in is dark brown like a coffee bean. My face is so shiny that I'm ashamed because I unwittingly defy conventions of beauty. I'm really not that bad-looking, but people don't see that. They simply look at this shiny-faced black girl, and they wish they don't see me. But sometimes they do.

They see my crinkly, kinky, unruly hair. The hair that laughs at neat ribbons and tidy barrettes. They see my long, skinny legs, interrupted only by a knobby, ashy knee, not unlike a giraffe, on each leg.

I remember sitting on the steps one day after Zelda had just called me an ugly, black spider. I remember everybody laughing and pointing at my ever-growing legs. I wouldn't let them see me cry, but my soul was paining me. I looked down at my legs and dreamed of all the places they would carry me some day. I dreamed and I dreamed until I dreamed the hurt away.

my inner self

My eyes are like burnt coal. They are so black that they match the night sky, the same one that the slaves must have seen through the cracks from the belly of the drifting beast. They say that the eyes reveal the soul, but nobody ever bothered to look into my eyes, so they never saw me or my inner self.

My inner self is beautiful. My inner self dances like Dagoberta. It sings like Sylvia. It leaps like Lydia. It moves like Maria. It somersaults like Selena. My inner self is so beautiful that I go there to stay when no one else wants me. I feel like the glorious beauty of my inner self should radiate outwards so that the world can see. But it doesn't, so they don't.

mi familia

I have two brothers and one sister. Caramia, my sister, is the oldest. She's fifteen years older than I am, and often it seems like I don't know her at all. Then, at other times, I know her well because I know my mother.

Freeman is twelve years older than I am. I've always loved his name. It sounds so solid, so strong. But he's weak. He used to rob old women, steal their purses, break into their houses, whatever. So he has spent a lot of time away.

My other brother is Sojourn. He's nine years

older, and I love him dearly, but he's a floater. He's rarely in the same place for long. He's always moving, searching. Unlike my mother, he's not running away. He's running to.

my tired mother

My mother is always tired. It's almost like she was born tired. As years go by, the rings under her eyes get darker. People normally don't notice subtle changes like that, but I do. That's the only clue of her age, those rings set in smooth skin the color of Georgia earth.

Every morning she awakens with a jump as if something has frightened her. She wipes the sweat from her face and walks over to the window, peering out as if she's looking for something. She searches the street first. Then she scans the sky, and she seems to be hoping.

She drags her body down the stairs, where she opens the refrigerator. There, in a shot glass, is her chilled-to-perfection vitamin that helps her start the day smoothly. Suddenly revitalized, she bounds back up the stairs, racing between the bedroom and the bathroom, getting ready to face the world. She smoothes makeup like cake batter under her eyes to hide the dark circles. Mask in place, she scampers down the stairs and to the front door. The door opens and closes, and then she's gone without even a good-bye.

Still running.

C

My mother cursed the school nurse who told her the news.

"She ain't got no damn curve in her back," she spat bitterly. "Ain't nothin' wrong with my child. Song, stand up straight to show this woman she don't know what the hell she talkin' bout."

I stood up, turned my back to my mother and the nurse, and looked at the blank wall before me. I tried hard to will my back straight. I really did, but I could tell by the way that my mother sucked her teeth that it was still crooked. I was still crooked.

"Song, I said stand straight," she snapped.

I sucked in my stomach and pushed and pushed my torso until I thought I was straight. The shadow on the wall told me I was no more straight than Quasimodo.

"She can't make herself straight, Mrs. . . ."

"That's Ms. Ms."

"Ms. Byrd, chastising her won't help. What will help is a brace. Since she's still young, a brace can help the problem."

By the way my mother looked at her, I could tell that she was no longer listening. I was, though. I wanted to hear about anything that would make me normal, more like the other kids.

". . . an appointment with a pediatrician so that she can be evaluated. If she doesn't have one, you can call one of the doctors on this sheet. Over time you'll begin to see . . ."

"Mm-hmm. Thank you. Sure, ma'am. Okay. Good-bye." My mother collected her things, me included, and was out the door before the nurse could finish her sentence.

As we walked through the door, I heard my

mother crumple up my hope for normal health and toss it into the trash can.

"Ain't nobody gon' tell me what to do with my child."

caramia's
concert

Her rich voice enveloped Marvin's words. Her thick lips framed the anguish in his voice. She closed her eyes and for that moment, she was in another place. Swaying back and forth, she wrapped her arms around herself, looking amazingly like a small child on the verge of tears.

When she opened her eyes, she saw me sitting on her bed, watching. Suddenly self-conscious, she began to talk while applying lip-liner. The more she talked, the more she relaxed. Soon, her laughter filled the room, and I felt happy. She kissed me on the nose and left.

I waited up for her because I wanted to hear how her concert was. When I heard the door open, I rushed to the top of the stairs to meet her. As I listened to her footsteps across the floor, something sounded different. As she came into view at the bottom of the steps, she looked different, too.

"Hey, little bit," she said. With her speech slurred, her words sounded like "little bitch." Instinctively, I recoiled, thinking of my mother.

She stumbled up the stairs, clutching her four-inch heels to her bosom. I wanted to talk to her, but when I saw her face, something stopped me. Her eyes were red and puffy, and her lipstick was gone. When she passed me, I smelled the same pungent odor that seeped from her room when my mother was not at home.

I crept back toward my bedroom door, watching her stumble down the hall and into her room.

"Goodnight, Caramia," I said to the darkness. Two weeks later, she moved out.

outside

They aren't always mean to me. In fact, sometimes we get along just fine, and they let me play with them. I like that, but I hate when they start picking on someone else. I never participate, but I feel guilty for my silence. Sojourn told me that some writer said that the hottest places in hell are reserved for those who, in times of crisis, do nothing. I don't consider it a crisis, but I don't want to go to hell either.

The clip-clop of the double-Dutch rope punctuated the spring air. The rhythmic chant of the accompanying song was almost inaudible beneath the music blaring from Miss Olga's second-floor window.

"I should go tell her to turn that down. I can't even concentrate," Zelda complained, angry because she had only gotten to twelve.

"I know," Lydia agreed. "That stuff is old-timey anyway."

Just then, as if she knew that her music was too loud, she turned it off, her long fingers flicking the switch.

"I thought so," Zelda said, lifting her T-shirt to let her stomach get a taste of the slight breeze stirring.

Miss Olga appeared in her door, an unlit cigarette dangling from her lips. She looked wistfully down the street, one hand to her chest like she was trying to keep her heart from breaking through her chest.

"Miss Olga," Zelda cooed sweetly, waiting for the heartbroken woman to face her. When their eyes locked, Zelda lowered the boom. "*Dónde está su esposo?*"

For a split second, that tiny amount of time it took to register that he was not here, Miss Olga looked sad. Then anger flashed through her, forcing her lips apart. The cigarette dropped from her mouth, and she turned so quickly to go back into the house that she almost fell off the steps.

Back inside, she turned on the radio again, its speakers facing the street. She turned up the music loudly to lure back the man with pink skin, who had loved her hard before shooting himself, and the daughter who, tired of missing her daddy, dove in the water in search of him.

when my
mother goes

I understand why she does it, but I hate myself for being so understanding. I hurt because I'm supposed to hurt. Because it's not a good thing. But instead, I forgive her because I know that she feels like she has no other option.

When my mother goes out at night, she locks me in the bathroom since there is no one to take care of me. The first time she did it, I cried and begged and begged and cried. I didn't want to stay in there because it's not a nice place. The water faucet on the sink doesn't work, so we use the bathtub to wash our hands, brush our teeth, and bathe. Roaches scamper out from behind the mirror and under the medicine cabinet. They hide themselves under towels and any other place they can fit. They march in formation when it's dark, which is quite often. The lights in the bathroom haven't worked for years, so the only way to see is through the skylight.

The skylight only opens about six inches, and when I'm locked in, I take advantage of that little space. From where I stand in the center of the bathroom, directly under the skylight, I can only see a little piece of sky. Even though it's small, I stare up and up and up, and I forget about the roaches and the lights and the water. I look at that little piece of sky, and I have hope.

anger

I feel it creeping in at the seams, but I try to stuff it back down. I don't want to let it in because if I do, it will rule my life.

I'm angry that my family is, by mainstream standards, dysfunctional. Around here, though, my situation is considered pretty normal, but in my heart I still feel what's right. I don't need some politician wagging his finger at me through the television screen, though, telling me how screwed up my environment is.

I'm angry that my sister shoots heroin and smokes crack every day. She steals into my mother's house and escapes with a sacrifice that she makes to appease the white-rock god. Anything will do. The vacuum cleaner. A lamp. An iron. A suitcase. The Barbie that Miss Olga gave me. Anything. When she can't get into the house, she kneels or lays down in alleyways, hoping to collect enough to pay Deacon "I-Got-A-Hold-On-You" so that he will disseminate the god's blessing upon her. I'm so angry at her that I want to forget my dear sister Caramia, but she won't let me go.

I'm angry that Freeman hates women, for he also hates me. I heard him curse a woman so badly one day that I cried. I'm angry that he won't ever change, and I feel that stronger than anything that I've ever felt before.

I'm angry that Sojourn just picks up and leaves me here. He goes away for weeks at a time, always sending me a postcard detailing the grand place that he's visiting. He returns with trinkets for me, but I must hide them from Caramia. I ask him why he can't take me with him, and he says that ten is too young to see the things he sees.

I'm angry that we all don't have the same father. Am I to believe that my mother is a whore? That's what the kids on the block say, but they hardly get a glimpse of her because she's always moving so quickly. Running.

I'm angry that I was a mistake. Nobody had to tell me that. I knew because of the big age difference between me and Sojourn. But just in case there was any doubt, my mother told me anyway. I'm angry with her.

c revisited

Sometimes I stand naked in front of the mirror, and I study my body. It's a plain-looking body. Nothing much to note. My face is darker than the rest of me. I wish I could somehow reverse that, you know, cover up the darkness that hangs on me like a leaden cape. The darkness is unwanted. It's worthless like the dark meat of the chicken, or the "black ball" that keeps people out and away from their desired ambitions.

When I'm not thinking about that, I'm reexamining my back and wondering why. I turn away from the mirror and peer over my shoulder to get a better look. Despite the C-shaped curve, it looks perfectly normal. It reminds me of a musical instrument, a bass that my music teacher brought in to school to show us. It was dark, shiny, and powerful, not in that blatant, in-your-face kind of way, but more of a latent, don't-mess-with-me-because-I-am-the-undercurrent-that-holds-this-whole-song-together kind of way. Then, just as I'm about to feel pretty, I remember that I'm not a bass. I'm a person. I'm a girl. The temporary strength that I was feeling begins to subside, and I wilt. Then, I notice my back again, and I think that it looks like I feel. It looks like it's trying to curve itself up into a ball and shrink unnoticed into oblivion.

miss olga's kitchen

Wisdom sits at the tables of Black women. It also occupies a seat at the tables of Latinas as well. Miss Olga, who battles her own demons, watched from the window as Zelda and the others took aim at me again.

"*Venga aquí,*" she said to me as she started down her front steps. "Go inside," she ordered, pointing at her door.

Before I reached the door, I heard Zelda yelp in pain. When I turned to look, I saw Miss Olga dragging her down the street by the ear. The sight of loudmouthed Zelda being humbled by someone she had written off set me off in gales of laughter.

Inside Miss Olga's, I examined the pictures that

lined the fake fireplace. I recognized a few as a young Miss Olga. In one black-and-white shot, she stood next to a white man who gazed lovingly at her while she held a large rose to her nose. In another shot, she sat with her back to his chest. Her hands were folded over her protruding belly, and his hands were over hers. With each photo, I traced Miss Olga's life with her husband, right up until his funeral. As I stared at a picture of Miss Olga standing in front of a closed casket, I thought of the saying that I had heard about it being bad luck to take a picture with a dead person because it doesn't allow their spirit to rest. When Miss Olga entered the house behind me, I was wondering if that applies if the casket is closed.

"Stop being nosy and come in the kitchen," she ordered.

I sat in the chair that Miss Olga pulled next to the stove while she rummaged through a drawer. The flame on the stove danced blue and flared up when Miss Olga slammed a straightening comb down on the eye. Wordlessly, she parted my hair and rubbed grease into my scalp. The searing heat of the comb nearing my scalp unnerved me, but I sat still for fear of being burned. Once she finished straightening, she began curling, her long, agile fingers moving the handles so that the barrels clicked.

When she finished, Miss Olga stood in front of me with a mirror. I couldn't believe how my hair looked. Where small, tight curls once reigned, straight hair with delightfully curled ends now resided. I didn't think my hair could ever look like this. I never took the time to try it, and certainly no one else ever did.

I looked at Miss Olga through a watery haze. Silently I stood and walked to the door. From the step I quietly said thank you to the first person to ever do an unconditional deed for me.

in a panic

In a panic my mother rushed into the house last night. From the locked bathroom I could hear her heels click across the front room to the dining room. The door to the breakfront opened, and dishes rattled just as someone started pounding on the front door.

Downstairs, a woman's voice growled, "I'll kill you before I let you have him, you black whore."

My mother unlocked the front door, and in a voice thick like ice, she said, "Get the fuck away from my house. If you come here again, I'll blow your head off."

Then, I heard no voice, perhaps because my

heart was pounding in my ears. I wanted to break through the door and run to my mother to comfort her. But when she unlocked the bathroom door and saw my tear-stained face, she said, "Stop that damn crying before I cut your throat."

a happy day

I awoke to the sound of nothing. No high heels racing furiously across the floor. No sister banging on the front door. No music blaring from cars cruising down the street. No shouting from neighbors. Nothing. It was a sweet nothing, too. Not like the nothing that fills the air before a big snowstorm. Nor was it like the nothing that surrounds you in the eye of a storm. Just plain, sweet nothing.

After brushing my teeth and washing my face, I pointed my feet toward the stairs and marched down the lopsided, splintery steps to the first floor. The smell of toast hung in the air, and I followed it to the kitchen. On the table sat one buttered, brown slice next to a banana and a glass of orange juice still cool to the touch. I remembered to drink the orange juice last, and as a result, I was spared the bitter blast that usually comes when toothpaste and orange juice mix.

Back upstairs, I ran my bathwater and shook out a towel while watching the water level rise. After dunking my toe in the tub, I was pleased to find the water just right. I settled in like an ice cube, only I didn't break, and I watched as more drops trickled from the faucet. When wrinkled sufficiently, I got out and dried off, careful to wipe up any drops on the floor.

After getting dressed, I walked to Miss Olga's.

"*Voy al mercado*," she announced.

I asked her if she needed anyone to carry her groceries back. She understood my "shy speak" and said, "Sure, I'd like the company."

At the market, we sniffed mangoes, squeezed papayas, and thumped melons. We argued with the butcher about the price of beef. He agreed to lower the price if Miss Olga would cook dinner for him. She smiled politely and said okay. When I looked at her hand hanging down at her side, I saw that she had her fingers crossed. I laughed and she laughed and the butcher laughed while handing her the package.

"*Mentirosa dulce*," he said.

She returned, "I'd rather be a sweet liar than a sour one."

On the way home, Miss Olga sang a Spanish song to me. I think she was making it up as she went along, but it didn't matter. I just loved the sound of her raspy voice.

I helped her unpack the groceries before flopping down in a chair to watch her cook. She continued to sing, filling the house with liquid beauty. Then, she stopped abruptly and sent me downstairs to get some pots and soil. When I came back up, she set me up at the table with newspapers, pots, soil, and seeds.

We worked together in the sweet sound of nothingness, filling our pots with rich, almost black soil. We sprinkled in the seeds and gently covered them with more of the dark soil. We drizzled water over them, and I was about to pick up the pots and put them in the windowsill when Miss Olga stopped me.

She clasped my hand and whispered something in rapid-fire Spanish over the pots filled with soil the color of my skin. Then we sat down for fruit salad.

A few weeks later, sprouts broke through, and we smiled, reflecting on a happy day.

i wish

I wish a lot of things were different. Like I wish we weren't poor like we are. Then we wouldn't have to live in such a cruddy neighborhood. Then again, there's something about the noise that my mother needs. It's like she can't bear the silence. Like noise-lessness will suffocate her. I wish I knew how come.

I wish I knew why my mother and her brother won't speak to each other. A few years ago he came over for Christmas dinner. Once the firewater got in their systems, they started fussing and cussing. He told her that she saw what was happening and he knew that she saw it. She maintained that she hadn't seen shit, and if he insisted on telling her what she saw, he was welcome to get the hell out and never come back. That's what he did, and now she has no family besides us. And we're not enough.

I wish I could be enough. I wish I could pull my mother into my arms and coax her story out of her. I wish I could make her talk to me about her past. Her pain. I wish I could make her show me the affection I crave. I wish I could hear her say, "I love you." I wish I could tell her that I love her without being pushed away. I wish I could be enough.

caramia's hustle

Gotta get it. Gotta get it.

"I'll watch your car so that nobody messes with it. You can pay me when you get back."

Gotta get it. Gotta get it.

"All I need is a little spare change to catch the subway home."

Gotta get it. Gotta get it.

"You need your windows cleaned?"

Gotta get it. Gotta get it.

"I just want to borrow your TV to watch the fight."

Gotta get it. Gotta get it.

"I'll hail a cab for you."

Gotta get it. Gotta get it.

"Just a few coins for food."

Gotta get it. Gotta get it.

"I'll wash your car for you."

Gotta get it. Gotta get it.

"Miss, I'll carry your groceries for you."

Gotta get it. Gotta get it.

"Mister, I think we can make a nice exchange."

Gotta get it. Gotta get it.

"Anybody wanna buy a VCR?"

Gotta get it. Gotta get it.

"Put your hands up."

Gotta get it. Gotta get it.

again in miss olga's kitchen

I sat at the table watching Miss Olga as she stared into a chipped teacup. She had been cooking dinner until I knocked on her door. When I walked into the kitchen and saw the big pot on the stove, I almost said, "Wow! You must be having a lot of company." Then I noticed the table set for three, and I remembered Miss Olga's husband and Maria, who missed her daddy so much that she dove into the water so that she could catch up with him.

Sitting in the empty place, I waited for Miss Olga to say something. When she looked up from her cup, she said, "Well, you came here. You must have something to say."

My mind raced as I tried to conjure words to my mouth.

"I got a postcard from my brother Sojourn today," I started.

"That's nice. Where is he?"

"He's in Massachusetts now. He says that he's working at this camp for the summer. He's working in the kitchen, cooking for a bunch of rich kids from around the world."

"It's honest work," she offered.

I shook my head, and my mouth was empty again.

"Song, what will you do when you get older?"

I had never entertained the thought of getting older. I certainly hadn't thought of what I would do. I shrugged my shoulders.

"My Maria wanted to run a foundation that provided help to kids and poor people."

I didn't know what a foundation was or what it took to run one, but on that day, there in Miss Olga's kitchen, I decided that I would find a foundation and run it so that Miss Olga would be happy.

a little piece of sky

I never have the heart to look up when I'm outside, but when I'm locked in the bathroom, that's what I do. Above the roaches, above the water spots, above the peeling paint, I can see a little piece of sky.

One evening while I was looking up, I heard it all unfold downstairs beneath my feet. My mother rushed in and scurried across the floor. She didn't close the door behind her, but rushed into the dining room and opened the breakfront. I could hear her jangling the dishes. I heard her curse and mumble, and then I realized that she was looking for the gun that she had kept hidden away in the soup tureen. But it wasn't there. I knew because I had taken it to my room to examine it one afternoon while my mother was sleeping. Then Caramia had come, looking for something to take to the altar. I didn't want her to wake my mother and upset her, so I had given the gun to her so that she could sell it. So that she could ease her pain.

Now, downstairs I heard a second voice. It shouted, "Didn't I warn you to keep your black ass away from him? You couldn't stay away. Now you will."

Then I heard a pop. Then a thud. Then feet calmly walking away.

I stood in the bathroom, screaming up at the sky. The sky that had betrayed me and my mother by giving us a false sense of hope. I screamed even after I heard the sirens outside, even after I heard the voices downstairs, even after Miss Olga shushed me from the other side of the door, until she kicked it in.

She looked at me with sadness in her eyes before reaching out to me. I resisted her arms because I needed confirmation. I needed to hear it.

With eyes as melancholy as a drooping African

violet, she told me. She said, "*Esta muerta, niña. Esta muerta.*"

And on that day, I vowed never to look up at the sky again because I do not deserve hope. I killed my mother.

azul

Azul.

It's the color of the deepest part of the ocean. The part where dreams sink and huddle together like skeletons from the Middle Passage.

Azul.

It's the color of Billie's voice. She had no choice. It just filled her body like a deadly gas.

Azul.

It's the color of a winter day when it's too cold to grow anything but stems of sadness, which are perennials.

Azul.

It's the color of the gumball that stains your tongue. It stains it so dark that people laugh, and you don't know why they are laughing at you. Then you think of the gumball and remember its deep shade.

Azul.

It's the color of poor Maria's lips as they pulled her from the pool where she dove in search of her father.

Azul.

It's the color of the vein that Caramia searches for.

Azul.

It's the color of loneliness.

Azul.

It's color of the bruise on your back when you thought that you were too dark for the beating to cause a mark.

Azul.

noon

here

Things are different here in my father's house.

Take the kitchen, for example. For one thing, the refrigerator does not have a lock on it, so I can go in it as often as I please. Once inside, there are no names taped to the food, prohibiting me from tasting something that looks especially scrumptious.

Here there are so many rooms that I could lose myself. The living room is huge, and the chairs all seem to be on the verge of bursting because they are stuffed so big. This is a sense of comfort that is so discomforting to me.

Here the lights don't go off because the bill can't be paid. I don't have to climb on the roof to rig an electrical cord to a neighbor's outlet for a temporary debt that my mother will have to pay on her back. I can flick a switch, and the room will flood with lights so bright that it seems like daytime.

Here I'm not awakened by loud music or gun shots or sirens or arguing or sisters coming to beg for money, promising that this is the last time. I awake with the sun or the sound of a gentle voice urging me to rise and shine and greet the day with a smile, but I don't because I'm not used to smiling yet. Everyone around me seems excited about the challenges that a new day will present. That's another switch from the gotta-get-up-and-face-the-man blues that's so much a part of tan, red, brown, and black lives.

Here I go to church on Sundays, where we pray and sing and rejoice. Fat ladies in all of their finery come up and pinch my cheeks, oblivious to my impatient looks. Old men sharp as tacks in three-piece suits and hats surrender themselves to an intangible but powerfully real God. I was beginning to think that God had forgotten about us. That S/He had gone on to start over on another planet because things on Earth have gotten so bad. But looking into the tear-stained faces of the ladies, I know that S/He is still here.

Here I'm given choices. What would you like for lunch? Do you want to go to the video store? Would you like to have some kids from school over? Let's go for a walk, shall we? I've never been given so many choices in my life. And it feels fine.

my father

I study him when he's not looking. While he's building a fire in the fireplace, while he's mixing tuna fish
for my lunch, while he's reading a magazine, I watch
him, and I wonder what's going through his mind. Is
he trying to stay busy so that he doesn't have to
think, just like my mother used to do? Is he trying to
stay busy so that he doesn't have to talk to me? I
wonder if he knows what it was like with my mother.
How we didn't have much money or food or other
basics. I try to hate him for that, but I always end up
liking him again when he looks up, and I see those
eyes so black that they match the night sky that the
slaves must have seen through the cracks from the
belly of the traveling beast. Those eyes like mine.

still angry

My new school is so different from my old school. It's hard to believe that this is a public school. The books are new, the desks clean. The teachers, even the old ones, are fresh. I really feel like I'm learning, and my A-average is confirmation of my thirst for knowledge. Even though I'm one of a few blacks in the school, they don't treat me badly. In fact, they pretty much leave me alone. All except one. Miss Turner, my English teacher.

She's one of five black teachers in the school, and most of the kids like her, despite the fact that she plays strictly by the book. That's where we butt heads. She's always riding me about wearing my jacket in the building. We're not supposed to, but nobody else says anything, so why does she have to? When I'm in her class, I slide it off my shoulders and onto my chair. Then, sometimes she asks me to go to the board for something, and I put my jacket back on. Walking to the front board, I can feel her eyes looking at me with contempt. Before I can get to the board, she yells at me to sit back down until I can follow the school's rules. I want to tell her that I want to follow the rules, but I'm ashamed of my C-shaped back. But she never asks, and I never offer.

"I want to know why you said that," she said, ignoring my desire to be left alone.

"Look at me."

I wanted to, but I was fighting tears and fighting myself.

She stood in front of me and lifted my chin, trying to make me meet her gaze.

"The only reason I haven't written you up is because I sense that something is wrong. Will you talk to me?"

I was in emotional withdrawal, missing *mi madre*. Scared of this new place, no matter how nice it is.

She waited while I thought. It's hard for me to open up. I haven't ever done it.

"I'm new here," I began.

"I know that, Song."

"I don't know how to . . . I'm new here," I started again. "I'm new to this."

Her eyes softened as she waited.

I couldn't continue.

Her eyes hardened again.

"Song, you just can't go around threatening people because they ask you to do something that you don't want to do. If you can't explain yourself, then I have no other recourse than to follow the normal procedures."

My eyes were steel. I stood.

"Do what you have to do," I said, and I walked out, carrying a weight that I wanted desperately to unload.

my friend

I'm friendly with this girl who lives down the street. Her name is Sloane, and she's already got a best friend named Romy, but I like to hang out with her anyway. She's pretty, and she's so ladylike that I feel like Mowgli from *The Jungle Book* next to her. That doesn't make me dislike her, though. In fact, I'd like to be more like her.

Sometimes we run together, but she's not really a runner like I am. She's a dancer, but she says that running helps to keep her legs toned. That's cool because I get to spend time with someone my own age, since my father and his wife don't have any other kids.

One evening Sloane and I were running, and something told me to look up to the top of this pole. The transformer at the top of the pole was on fire, and blue flames shot to and fro. Sloane panicked and froze, while I ran to the first house I saw. I banged on the door until a man answered. He looked at me like I smelled, but I ignored that. My words tumbled out.

". . . fire on top of the pole . . . blue flames . . . afraid that something will happen to the house near it . . ."

After he pushed his skepticism aside, he pushed open the screen door, and we rushed down his walkway. By the time we joined Sloane in the street, the flames were dying, and the people who owned the house near the burning pole had come home.

Looking up, we saw that the fire was now gone, and happy chatter passed between the neighbors. The man asked us our names, and after we told him, he said that he was going to send a note to the community paper about our heroism.

"You girls have done a good deed," he said, reaching out and pulling honey-colored Sloane to him in an embrace. Over her shoulder, he looked at me like I wasn't there. After releasing her, he turned his back and returned to his house, leaving my jaw hanging slack in my black face.

back in miss olga's kitchen

I felt somehow different as I walked down Fifth Street in my old neighborhood. The bicolored sidewalk swirled blue and green before me, and each step I took was smaller than the one before, as if I were walking toward a place where I didn't want to be.

I stood on the steps with raised fist, wondering if Miss Olga would recognize me. I wondered if five years had changed my appearance as much as they had changed my mind.

Miss Olga opened the door and said, "No sound will come if you don't actually knock."

Still the same Miss Olga.

"How are you doing, Miss Olga?"

"Not as fine as you," she said, pulling me inside. "I see you're keeping your hair up."

Self-consciously I touched my hair, nervous that one of the ever-present peas might jump out.

"You look like you're standing straighter."

"I've been wearing a brace to help correct my back."

"It's really working."

We fell into place like familiar puzzle pieces. She filled my head with the goings-on in the neighborhood while she filled a plate, not one of the three already in place, with beans and rice.

"Your brother's out," she said, shaking her head. Without her saying a word, I knew that he was back up to the same old stuff. "I'm surprised he hasn't contacted you. I guess it's for the best."

I hadn't seen Freeman since my mother's funeral, when he was allowed out for two hours. I had thought about him from time to time, but I never had the desire to write or call him.

Miss Olga looked at me over her plate. "Do you miss him?"

"Not really," I said. "It sounds cold, but I never really had much of a life with him."

"Do you wish you had?"

"If it means that I would have turned out like him, no."

i thought

I always thought that my mother was so brave, raising children on her own. I thought that she had heart, going out into the cold world every day, battling to put food on the table. The men who left her, they were cowards. They did their business in the cloak of darkness, and stepped out on her, my intrepid, unflinching mother. But now I think differently.

Now that I know Faith, my father's wife, I know what courage is. She tried for years to have a baby, but God didn't give her one. I think that she probably felt like less than a woman, so she turned a blind eye to my father's philandering. When I arrived after I killed my mother, she accepted me with open arms.

Any other woman would have walked away from the pain and the man who caused it. She stuck it out and fought for her man, showing him and others that the brave thing is to love.

sojourn's postcard

It read,

> *Hey, little sister. I hope all is well. I'm in Crisfield, Maryland. The water called to me, and here I am. I'm working on a shrimp boat. My days are long, and they start early, but I'm not in a rush to get home to anybody, so I don't mind.*
>
> *It's beautiful down here. Once in a while when I'm out on the water rocking back and forth, I find myself on the verge of tears. I don't really know why, but I think it's because something's missing, only I don't know what it is.*

Maybe the water will speak to me, and I'll find the answer.

Truly,

Sojourn

our adventure

"We want to get a taste of life in the 'hood," Romy said. "Take us to your old neighborhood."

I looked at Sloane, the more sensitive of the two, hoping that she would intervene. I hoped that she would say that it wasn't a good idea. I hoped that she would say that being poor isn't a late afternoon excursion. Being poor isn't a view through a rolled up window of a luxury car. Being poor isn't something that you can turn on and off at will. But Sloane said nothing, so into Romy's BMW we piled, heading south on Broad Street, away from West Mt. Airy wealth.

"Make a left here," I heard myself say, navigating my way back to hell.

"Here we go," Romy said, grinning with mischief.

I caught Sloane's eye in one of the mirrors of the sleek car. I tried to keep the pleading out of my eyes, but I guess I couldn't because Sloane shifted her gaze.

"Girl, we can probably find us some real men down here," Romy oozed. "Like him." She nodded her head in the direction of Juaquin, Zelda's brother, who was standing on the corner. Zelda's brother, who has six kids by five different women. Zelda's brother, who has a hit out on him because he dropped the dime on one of the Eighth and Butler hustlers. Zelda's brother, who dropped out of school in eighth grade. Zelda's brother, who will die soon, leaving six children, six brothers and sisters, to be raised by five different women.

"*Papi's* got edge," Romy giggled. "He reminds me of your cousin Gerald."

Sloane responded, "Gerald was like that before getting locked up. He's changed. You know that."

Romy ignored her, intent on exploring the "dark" side of the city. This was an adventure to her. A mission she would never truly understand, nor would she ever even try.

And as she glowed, I faded.

caramia

Caramia had a baby, and she was born too soon. She said she didn't know she was pregnant. She said that when her periods stopped, she thought it was because of the drugs. Four months, she went. Four months with no periods. Then stomach pains crippled her. She crawled to Miss Olga's house, and together they went to the hospital, where she gave birth to a child who quivered and thrashed and shrieked her way into our consciousness.

It had been easy to forget about Caramia, but who can forget a quivering child? There, in the hospital, she begged God to help her get herself together so that she could be a good mother. She prayed that the baby born five months too soon would make it, but the chances of that looked slim. God knew better than the doctors, though, and let the little baby girl live. Because she didn't have a home, Miss Olga took Caramia and the baby to her house. The little girl, who Miss Olga named Maria, needed special attention. My sister tried. Lord knows she tried, but guilt drove her back out into the streets. You would think that Miss Olga would be mad, but she didn't bat an eye. She simply cleared the three place settings from the table, breathed deeply, and thanked God for a second chance.

judgment day

I sneaked in and sat in the last row of the courtroom. From where I was sitting, I could only see the top of Freeman's head. It wasn't that the room was especially crowded that day, although interest in the case was rather high, but he just looked so small and helpless. Like a kid.

I was thinking about how his life had fallen to such depths that he would rape a seventy-two-year-old woman. I was thinking about how the rage collected in him had consumed him so much that he had broken her right hip when he slammed her to the ground. I was thinking that my tiny family was so fragmented and splintered that I barely recognized them.

My brain was stirring all of these thoughts around when a voice reached in and shook me up.

"Freeman Byrd, on the count of sexual assault, I sentence you to ten years in the state penitentiary at Graterford."

I didn't tremble with emotion. I didn't let out a shriek. I didn't cry one tear. Instead, I looked up and into the judge's stern face, and I recognized him as the man who I had called out to see the transformer burning at the top of the pole that time when Sloane and I were running. He had judged me then. Today, he judged my brother.

mi padre

Surprisingly, conversation comes rather easily between us. In the beginning, we had our awkward moments, but then I figured that Faith and I got along so well, I should be able to get along with him just fine.

I actually learned a lot from him. He taught me how to read the stock pages and balance a checkbook. He taught me how to check the fluids and change the oil in my car, which was a present for my sixteenth birthday. He taught me how to make lemon meringue pie and cheesecake from scratch. And he also taught me about my mother.

"Song," he said one day. "Did you know that your mother could sing?"

I stopped grating lemon peel and racked my brain for a time when I heard my mother sing. I couldn't think of one. The only time she lifted her voice was when she was hollering at me.

"No, I didn't know that," I responded, returning to my lemon zest.

"She used to sing in church when she first moved to North Philly. She used to bring folks to tears," he said, checking my egg whites. "Well, that's what she said," he added. "By the time I met her, she hadn't set foot inside of a church for years."

I wasn't sure if I wanted to hear what he was saying, but for some reason, he needed to say it, so I didn't interrupt.

"She attended that church at Ninth and Ontario. The preacher used to compliment her singing and all, and pretty soon, he started sniffing around her. I imagine that she was flattered and all, with him being a man of the cloth and so prominent in the community. She invited him to her home and to her bed. The next thing you know, Caramia pops up. She said that the reason why she named the child that was because after a while, the reverend just called her 'my

77

dear,' like he forgot her name. Anyway, once Caramia was born, and the elders of the church didn't see any husband around, they called her to repent for her sinful ways. She had to walk to the front of the congregation and ask them for forgiveness. What added insult to injury was the fact that the reverend never parted his lips on her behalf. He never acknowledged that child."

With my pie in the oven, there was nothing else for me to do but listen.

"After she left the church, she needed something to occupy her time, so she started to hang with some civil rights folks. You know, she worked behind the scenes. She always was a hard worker. She got involved with one of the leaders. That's when Freeman came in. She started trying to flex her muscles some, get some respect. But many of those civil rights folks were hard-core sexists, and they couldn't deal with a strong woman stepping out of her place. She got ostracized, and that guy she was dealing with never tried to stand up for her. He was afraid to go against the grain. So that was that."

I was uncomfortable learning so much about my

mother. Things I never knew and never even suspected. I got up to check on the pies in the oven. I remained by the stove, waiting for him to continue.

"Sojourn's daddy wasn't worth a damn. He was there one day and gone the next."

He wiped his hands emphatically, like he was saying, "Good-bye and good riddance."

I looked at him with tears behind my lids. "What about my daddy?"

He sighed and sat back in his chair. His hands glided across the table and back again. After clearing his throat, he spoke.

"Your daddy fell in love with your mother. When he first saw her, she was standing alone on stage in a jazz club. Music was pouring out of her body, and the room was thick with the sadness and the pain flowing from between her lips. When she finished her set, your father was waiting for her by the alley where he knew she'd go to take a smoke. She had that scratchy roughness about her voice that all smokers have. Your father, not knowing that woman from Eve, took your mother in his arms and hugged her. She didn't even try to push him away.

Your father rocked her and rocked her there in the darkness of the alley. He heard her murmur, 'I ain't got nothin' left to give. I gave my love. I gave my heart. All I got is my song.' Your father didn't bat an eye. He said simply, 'And what a beautiful song it is.'"

The tears hit before I could leave the room. Now I know that all my mother wanted was to love and be loved.

my greek
ancestor

In school I read the story of Oedipus. Had I been Greek, he might have been one of my ancestors. Those deformed feet carried him far, but not far enough to be free. Just like my mother, and come to think of it, just like Sojourn.

The truth, or suspected truth as was the case, was too much for Oedipus to face. So he consulted the oracle for answers, just as my mother consulted the Ninth Street fortune-teller and Sojourn asked some chick on the Psychic Phone Line. None of them got satisfactory answers, but the prediction made for Oedipus was even more tragic. He was told that he would marry his mother after killing his father. Boy, I sure hope that it's not fated for me to marry my father. I've already fulfilled the first part of the prophecy. Maybe I should start running, too. But what would be the point? The story of Oedipus tells us that we can never escape who we are. We can never outrun our fate. Does that mean that we never try?

these feet attached to skinny legs

These feet attached to skinny legs have slapped barefooted on a dirty wooden floor. They have stepped over used syringes. They have scampered into the house away from would-be bullies. They have scurried away from bad places that threatened to suck me in.

They have stumbled up marble stairs in my father's house. They have soared over hurdles on the track. They have skidded through the sand at the end of the long jump. They have strutted down the aisle at my high school graduation. They have sauntered across the stage to accept my diploma as the first Byrd woman to graduate.

Now these feet attached to skinny legs will stride through the halls of Spelman College. They will be shaped by the steps of those sisters who came before me. They will set me on the path to a promising tomorrow.

azul ii

Azul.

It's the color of the cotton candy your father buys you at the Mt. Airy Day carnival in Sedgwick Park. It's your first carnival, and as you stuff yourself with hot dogs and funnel cake, you make sure to leave room for the sweet cotton candy.

Azul.

It's the color of the sweet-sixteen party dress that you got from Faith. It makes you old, yet young. Sensual, yet sweet.

Azul.

It's the color of your first car. Although it's a little dull because you got it used, you wax it and buff it until it shines like new.

Azul.

It's the color of the tiny footsteps you take around your room just because you can. The carpet is so plush that you can almost sink in it, so you dive onto the bed, which is soft like a cloud.

Azul.

It's the color of the blanket you use when you go on weekly picnics with your new family. You sit in the middle, and you imagine that you are drifting along on water. Then, you remember poor Maria whose father left her, and you are sad and scared.

Azul.

Sometimes it's the color of fear.

Azul.

saturday

They are used to the routine. Yet they still attempt to stand strong. All of them stand strong. Thousands of them stand strong. All of them, black and thick, stand strong against the oppressive whiteness. They fight because they don't know how not to. When it looks like they are down for the count— one, then, two, then, five, then, ten—they all spring back up. They stand defiantly, facing the oppressive whiteness that threatens to lay them out for certain. Kill them dead. They hate to endure it, and I hate to watch it. But another revolution will come in six weeks. I'd rather not spend my Saturdays locked in a beauty shop getting a relaxer.

now

Like I promised Miss Olga all those years ago, I work for a foundation. I started working for them right after I graduated from Spelman, and I've been here just over two years. I like my job because we do good work. I wear many hats. For example, I visit camps and recreation centers in areas like where I grew up, and I see what programs they have going on. Then I see if I can justify giving them the amount of money that they request. I always approve the requested amount because in neighborhoods like those, the people always need help and hope. When I visit, I usually find a reason to stay around there for a few days because I'm most comfortable with cream, gold, bronze, and brown people. I'm a part of them just as they are a part of me.

Another aspect of my job is to plan some of the fund-raising events. This is very different from visitation, but I enjoy it also. For some reason, even though I plan lavish galas, spectacular balls, and other elegant events, I never attend. I never feel like I belong there. Those people all have a lot of money to throw around. Me? I'm compensated very nicely at work, but I feel like I have nothing in common with them. I wonder if I'll outgrow this feeling.

healing

I knew that I needed to get some help.

It's hard for us to admit that we need help. You know, there's that whole Strong Black Woman facade to maintain. I simply can't deal with it. I'm not close to the edge or anything, I just know that I need some help undoing some of the damage done. I know that I deserve it, the help, but something in me says that it's trivial. It's frivolous. The voice says, "Think about all of those who came before you. Did they have help getting over? Think about the slaves. Was there a group therapy session just after the reading of the Emancipation Proclamation?"

I think about it, and Lord knows, if anybody needed it they surely did. They needed to deprogram generations of physical damage and self-hate that was poured into them. Surely if they can move beyond that, I can move beyond a few occasional beatings, poverty, and some bad names, right? Right?

hair

I've fought with my hair for years. From the time that I was a little girl, the battle of the tight tendrils has raged on, and I've done just about everything I can do to lay those suckers down. From Miss Olga's weekly press-'n'-curl and Faith's monthly relaxer treatments to the braided hairstyles I wore in college and the weaves I currently use for camouflage, I've tried it all.

When I think about it, it really is a waste. Why spend all kinds of time, money, and energy covering up the courageous little curls that God gave me? Nothing's going to keep them from coming, so I might as well let them come and be done with it. Just like Oedipus, I can't outrun it. Until I decide what to do, the battle will continue.

lunch with freeman

I don't know how I imagined it. I guess I thought it would be like some *Cosby Show* reunion, but it wasn't.

He had left a telephone number for me at Miss Olga's house. I called, and it turned out to be a halfway house. I remember thinking, "Okay, he's out again. Maybe this time he'll stay out."

We met at a soul-food spot on South Street, away from the hustle of Center City and the prying eyes of my co-workers. I was sitting in the booth a full twenty minutes before he showed up. He was bulkier than when I had last seen him. His eyes were quicker, almost jumpy. He had two scars under his right eye from being hit with a bottle, he told me.

Tattoos decorated his muscular forearm and corn-rows covered his scalp. His skin glistened in a way that reminded me of a polished-up slave on the block. When he opened his mouth, I saw that one of his front teeth had been chipped.

"Baby Sis," he said, grinning.

"Hey, Freeman," I returned, feeling uncomfortable because he looked so bad.

"You lookin' fine," he commented.

Wordless, I smiled and looked down at the plastic tablecloth under my arms. I was suddenly conscious of the way it was sticking to my skin because of nervous perspiration.

"So what's your plan?" I asked when my throat opened after the choking silence.

"I guess I gotta become a respectable member of society. Gotta get a gig. Settle into a nice little corner of the world. They hirin' at your job?"

He had absolutely no idea of what my job was, let alone where it was.

I shook my head. "Maybe they're hiring at the Ben Franklin Bridge," I said.

"Aw shit, tolls?" he asked, his eyes gleaming

at the thought of working near that amount of money.

"Mm-mm. There's a waiting list for toll collectors."

"Well how'd you get it?" he asked. I saw that his insecurities were rising to this surface when he thought that I was holding out on him.

"I was summer help. Don't you remember? They hired college kids in the summer so that regulars could go on vacation. They only gave us half the pay," I recalled.

"But your half was better than the average brother could get."

I felt his resentment for women creeping out. Although I knew that I would never be one of his victims, I didn't want to foment any anger in him.

We ate in relative silence for there was nothing to say. What was I supposed to ask about? The changes in the prison environment from his first visit to this most recent visit? Then I thought about it. Freeman had spent more time behind bars than he had outside.

Before I left I promised to look into a maintenance job at the bridge for him.

the barber shop

I surrendered the weave. My head felt a whole lot lighter. I never knew how much hair can weigh a person down. When I took the tracks out, despite its tightly curled texture, I could tell that my hair had thinned significantly after wearing weaves for so long.

I stood in front of the mirror for almost an hour, pulling, twisting, and poking at the mass atop my head. I washed it, then observed how it shriveled under the water. Then a realization hit me. No other hair can do that. There are numerous devices and products to straighten all kinds of hair, but no other hair will pull itself into ringlets so tight that they form a personal pillow.

I threw a baseball cap on my head and drove to the barber shop on Stenton Avenue. It wasn't crowded, so I sat in the first chair I saw. I told the barber to take me down so that my hair cuddled my scalp. He laughed and went to work with scissors until, thirty minutes later, he held up a mirror in front of me. I was shocked but pleased when I beheld my image. It seemed that, along with my hair, my barber had clipped away much of the anxiety I carried because my hair didn't cascade. Now, I looked at myself and thought that maybe my natural self wasn't so bad-looking after all.

healing ii

I called the National Association of Black Psychologists today. I didn't want to call my insurance company because I don't want anybody to link me with a shrink. It's silly, I know, but . . . I don't want to be labeled.

Anyway, the phone call was hard to make. First, I disguised my voice. Then I asked for the names of some therapists with practices near my Germantown apartment. The receptionist asked me if she could fax me the list, and, of course, I said no. How would I look, hanging around the fax machine waiting for a list of people who treat crazy folks? It took a while, but I got the names and numbers of about ten therapists.

Since I've been home, I've looked at the list, which is sitting on my kitchen table. I keep walking past it, hoping that something will happen. I don't know what, but something. Nothing does. I guess I have to make the next move.

maria

"You look like a boy," Maria said as she opened the door.

"Thank you," I returned, pinching her cheek.

Miss Olga stood at the back door fanning herself.

"*Hola*," I said, walking over to kiss her on the forehead. "You're shrinking."

"I'm old. That's what I'm supposed to do."

"*No es vieja*," I said, shunning her words. "*Es más joven.*"

"Ain't nothin' young on me but this new hair dye. How does it look?"

"*Muy bonita*. Very pretty. So what's happening?"

"Your niece is going to be the death of me."

"What's the matter?" I asked, pulling out a chair at the table.

"She's hungry. She's hungry for answers, and I don't know what to tell her."

"What does she want to know?"

"She wants to know about her family. She wants to know who that lady is who comes around banging on the door late at night, asking for money."

"I didn't know Caramia was bothering you. I'll sit vigil with you tonight. Then, tomorrow we're going to a realtor to find you a place closer to me."

"I'm too old to move," she whined. "Besides, this is my home."

"It's my home, too, but the neighborhood is changing and sometimes we have to let go," I reasoned, looking at her. That hair dye really was too dark for her light skin. I made a mental note to pick up another color, something light, on the way to the realtor.

"Let's go for a walk," I suggested.

"Okay, I'll close up the house."

The three of us rode in silence to Kelly Drive, and I parked on the circle behind the Art Museum.

"You two go ahead. I don't walk so fast no more," Miss Olga said.

I linked arms with Maria and bought two bottles of water from the man who sells snacks from his van while his fat dog lounges on a mattress in the shade.

"Do you know why you're named Maria?"

"Mm-mm."

"Miss Olga had a husband who loved her, and together they had a daughter. The husband died, and Miss Olga was sad. The daughter died in a drowning accident, and Miss Olga was even sadder. She grieved hard. For years she kept the table set for three, hoping that they would come back to her."

"That's stupid. How could they come back if they were dead?"

"Don't interrupt. She was just really sad, and she wouldn't let that go. She started looking after me, and I think that I helped her through that. But when you came, she finally cleared off that table and opened her arms to you. You're named after her daughter."

"That's creepy. But where did I come from?"

I sighed. "You came from my sister, Caramia."

" 'My dear?' "

"Mm-hmm. She was beautiful. She had a heart of gold, but she let a lot of things get to her. She took the easy way out."

I took a gulp of water and stopped walking. I turned her around to face me.

"That woman who comes around banging on the door at night is my sister, your mother, Caramia Byrd."

Tears began falling from her eyes. I wiped her face and pulled her further along on the walking path.

"I know it doesn't feel good, but that beautiful sister I love is still there. One day you'll see."

"I want to see tonight."

"Are you sure?" I questioned.

"Yes."

That night we sat in the kitchen eating fajitas. At eleven o'clock, someone started knocking on the door. Miss Olga looked at me and took a deep breath. I pushed myself from the table and walked to the door as the second round of pounding began.

"Come in here and quit all that banging," I commanded. I could tell that she was shocked to see me. I was sad because she looked so bad.

"What'chu doin' here?"

"I wanted to see you."

"What for?" she asked. She was talking fast, and by the way she was fidgeting, I could tell she was feinding.

"Your daughter wants to see you."

"I ain't got no daughter."

I slapped her hard. "Don't you ever say that. You have a daughter, and she's sitting at that table in the kitchen. So you're going to take yourself in that kitchen and say something to her."

In the kitchen, Maria played with her tortilla, sopping up the chicken grease and dragging it around her plate.

Caramia stood in the doorway looking at her child. "Hi," she said.

Maria looked up and said, "I love you." Just like that.

All of us stood in stunned silence.

"I love you because you made me. I know you have problems now, but when you get yourself together, Aunt Song, Mama Olga, and I will be waiting for you. Now get out of here and don't come back around here asking for money."

Then she got up and walked up the stairs to her bedroom.

"*De las bocas de los niños*," Miss Olga said after Caramia left.

"You said it, Miss Olga. From the mouths of babes."

the ball

I got talked into going. I really didn't want to go, but one of my co-workers reminded me that it doesn't look good not to show up at things. "Besides," she said. "You did most of the planning. You might as well enjoy the fruits of your labor."

I found a simple evening suit to wear, something understated but elegant. No gowns for me. I'm still self-conscious about my back even though most of the curve is gone.

I forced myself to socialize, but I couldn't sustain it. I'm really too shy for this sort of thing. Then, of course, I have this fear—of saying the wrong thing. I can just imagine that an inappropriate comment will tumble out of my mouth, and everyone will stare at me, dumbstruck. They would realize that I don't belong, and they would banish me back to the area of the city where the elevated trains ramble along, noisy enough to drown out my stupid words.

When the anxiety proved to be too much, I lingered by the hors d'oeuvres table under the guise of seeing what needed replenishing.

"You should try one of these," I heard a voice say.

I was tempted to ignore it, but I knew that it wouldn't be good form.

"Yes, everything is delicious," I responded, not looking up.

He wouldn't go away. "Would you like to try one?" he offered, the tongs proffered.

"Thank you," I replied, hurrying to shove the filo-wrapped shrimp in my mouth so that he would leave me alone.

"What do you think?"

Damn! Will he ever go? I thought before responding.

"It's very good."

"Well, if you like that, I'm sure you'll like this." He continued down the table, plucking delights from trays and presenting them to me. Even though I had sampled everything before at a tasting, somehow it tasted different this time. Better.

When he reached the end of the table, he offered me a napkin. Then he offered me his hand.

"Anthony Bella," he said. I admired his self-assurance.

"Song Byrd," I returned.

He smiled before asking, "Do you sing?"

"Not a lick," I said, grinning back.

While we talked, I noticed the golden glow of his skin and mentally contrasted it with my own dark skin. His hazel eyes seemed to bore into me. Through me. His hair formed a curly frame around his face, and his teeth looked like chips of opal set between his succulent lips. I had to fight the urge to kiss him, which was very odd considering that I had just met him.

We walked out onto the balcony where the air was incredibly clear.

"The stars are brilliant," he commented.

"Mm-hmm," I agreed, not looking up. I hadn't looked at the sky in years, and I didn't intend to start now.

We talked for hours, and before I knew it, the jazz band had stopped playing.

"Well, the music has stopped. I guess it's time to go," I said, still inhaling the air, intoxicated by its purity.

"I still hear a beautiful song," he ventured.

After a while, he walked me to my car, where he hugged me goodnight.

"I'll call you tomorrow at noon," he promised.

I disregarded his comment as a polite good-bye, but the next day at noon, the phone rang. As I sat on the balcony of my apartment, I breathed deeply, and I almost looked up.

dreaming

I've been dreaming a lot lately, and most of my dreams involve my mother.

Most of the time I don't remember much about them, but I try to scribble down a few thoughts when I awaken, before the thoughts, like my mother, are lost to me.

Some of the words on my notepad, which I keep by the bed, are "floating up," "running away," "gun," "fault," "find peace," and "sorry."

I'm not sure what any of this means. I probably won't know until I get to a therapist. He can probably help me sort some of it out.

Oh, yeah. I've decided to make an appointment with a male doctor because I figure that he can provide more logical, sound advice. For all I know, choosing a male therapist is probably another one of my hang-ups. It's probably some kind of unresolved paternal conflict. You know, some quest to make my father hear me.

Sheesh, I need help.

miss olga's friend

Miss Olga had a friend, but she died. She asked me to go with her to the funeral. I agreed because now Miss Olga seemed so frail, and I hate to see the frail stand alone.

After viewing the casket, Miss Olga turned her nose up, but she didn't cry.

"That's not her," she said. "That's not my Linda."

"What do you mean?" I asked.

"My Linda was round, full, and she had a face that laughed even when her lips did not. That woman there is a stick. She's not Linda. That stick is not my Linda."

She pointed to the grieving man on the front row. "He did it. He killed her," she said loudly.

"Shh," I warned, wondering if I'd have to take her out of the church.

The more Miss Olga talked, the more I realized that Linda's husband had killed her. He murdered her spirit.

Linda had worked as a secretary in his architectural firm. After they got married, he insisted that she quit her job, which she loved. Seeking something to fill her endless hours, she joined clubs and sat on boards, and it seemed to fill her. Miss Olga went to work as her servant, but she suspected that the woman simply wanted the company of another tan face in her white world. Miss Olga would cook and together they would have grand lunches and talk and laugh until her husband came home. Late. Every night late. After lunch, Linda dialed the phone, leaving messages for fellow club members, the friends who were no friends.

Her husband gave all of himself to the world during the day, leaving nothing for his wife. He courted clients, smiled when appropriate, giving them everything his wife needed. By the time he got home, there was nothing left for the beautiful Linda.

One day when Miss Olga was too sick to work, Linda asked her husband, "Honey make me some beans and rice."

"I don't want to eat that," he said.

"I do. You can use one of those prepackaged recipes, but make me some beans and rice."

He got up and went into the kitchen. Fifteen minutes later he returned with a plate of angel hair with meat sauce. She ate it quietly, and as soon as she was finished, she went to the bathroom and threw it back up behind a closed door. She called Miss Olga that night and told her not to come back. Linda continued to pay her, though, until she found a new job.

Miss Olga checked on her from time to time, and, at each visit, there seemed to be less and less of Linda, who said that she needed to lose a few pounds. When a few turned into sixty, Miss Olga begged to come back so that she could take care of her. Linda wouldn't let her, though. She continued her routine of having juice with her husband in the mornings before he left for work. She drank broth for lunch and had nothing for dinner. When her husband returned home in the night, he always found her in bed. She pretended to be asleep, but really she had no energy to function and no desire to keep living alone in the house where her husband resided.

The friends who were no friends came to see her, this ninety-pound woman. She laughed at them, and told them to leave her alone.

And that is how she died. Alone in a room full of things, in a bed next to a weeping mate who was no mate.

As Miss Olga leaned down during the final viewing, she whispered, "*Vaya con Dios, Linda. El te comprende.*"

sojourn's postcard part ii

Dear Song,

I'm in South Dakota, and all is well. I'm
on a reservation, teaching adults to read.
They're teaching me to live. We often think
that we've had it so bad. But before we arrived
in shackles, these people, our red brothers and
sisters, walked freely. I don't remember seeing
any walking freely around Sixth Street.

It's beautiful out here. As I sit here writing
to you, all around I see uninterrupted earth.
Vast expanses of sandy-colored ground. It sure
is pretty, but I don't know how long I'll be here.
I miss the water.

Have you seen Caramia?

How's our niece? Don't let her wear Miss Olga out.

Signing off from SD and sending you much love,

Sojourn

the judge

The yellow light glared at me as I approached the busy intersection. As I pressed the brakes, the lunch that I was bringing Anthony slid forward on the seat. I leaned over and placed the package on the floor, and when I sat back up, I saw him, standing on the corner, waiting to cross the street in front of my car. The judge.

I recognized him instantly. The clipped mustache perched above cruel, thin lips. In his hair, a conservative bush, glinted silver strands. His face was unchanged. It was still hard, set in a perpetual scowl, as if he couldn't understand why he should be forced to walk among the commoners. He was supposed to be able to fly. Didn't the gods know this? What was the delay in his getting his wings?

As he stepped off of the curb, my dark hands gripped the steering wheel harder. Had I been lighter, my knuckles would have blanched from the pressure. Had I been lighter, I probably would not have held contempt for this man, the judge, who had judged me unworthy and had judged my brother unfit. Subconsciously, he probably lumped us all together. The dark ones who were a drain on the race.

He tread cautiously across the street, carrying a Lenox bag. I imagined that the cream-colored sculpture inside fit perfectly into his cream-colored world. Once at home, he would unwrap it and dust it, making certain that no ugly dark specks came to rest on it.

I felt my foot slipping from the brake as he stepped in front of my car. I fought back the bad memory, and I fought off the bad feelings just in time to put my foot back on the brake pedal. And I let the judge live even though he had made my dark innocence die all those years ago.

healing iii

I finally made it to a therapist's couch. After all of my stalling, I finally lay down and began to disman-tle the wall that was blocking me in.

I didn't know what to say. I told him that I didn't want him to think of me as some nutcase. I told him that I am a professional woman who simply has a lot on her plate. I told him that I didn't need therapy. I just needed somebody to help me sort through some of my thoughts.

He told me that I shouldn't feel any shame in coming to talk to him. He told me that everybody needs a time and place to unburden themselves. He told me that a lot of Black people hold on to this idea that therapy is only for the rich. He told me that I have nothing to be ashamed of.

I agreed. Then I paid the receptionist in cash so that my insurance company could not link me to the shrink.

with anthony

I spend Saturday afternoons with Anthony at his store on Jewelers' Row. It's called Bella Jewels, and his parents set him up in it after he graduated from Hampton four years ago. He loves what he does, and he takes pride in his store.

His cousin Chauncey works with him, but on weekends Chauncey goes fishing, so I come in and help. I really don't do much, but Anthony tells me how glad he is that I'm there. So I keep coming around.

I like it when the store is empty because then I try on some of the jewelry. I feel like a princess when I'm adorned in the jewels. The first time I tried a necklace on, I thought I was being slick.

Anthony was in the back when I slid the case open and removed the necklace. After fastening the clasp around my neck, the diamonds set in the white-gold necklace came to life. They sparkled and shone so much that I grew dizzy from their brilliance. I admired myself for a few minutes before returning it to the case.

When Anthony emerged from the back, he kissed me on the cheek, and whispered in my ear, "As bright as those diamonds glitter, they don't compare to your smile."

I was embarrassed that he had seen me in the security camera, but he said, "Don't be. If anyone deserves jewels, you do."

It would be so nice to believe him. Maybe I will.

two worlds

For a long time now, I've been caught between two worlds, and it's not easy.

In one world people are self-sufficient and motivated. They make a way for themselves, and they're not afraid to try. They know that not trying is tantamount to true failure, and that failure is simply a learning experience. They know that their ideas have worth, and they want to make their worth known.

In the other world, the people are different. Though they seem to be content with nothing, they actually are not. They are simply afraid. The world has told them that they will never amount to anything, that their ideas are stupid. The ideas are not stupid, but the people are stupid, for they believed the world rather than believing in themselves.

In the first world, there are luncheons and auctions, galas and premiers. There are no price tags because you simply go after what you want and you get it. There are lazy afternoons under Caribbean sun and gusts of cold air on a wintry slope. There is always enough, but there can never be too much because it's all there for your taking.

In the second world, there are Chinese food joints where the proprietors greet you from behind three-inch walls of Plexiglas. There are businesses that make you pay three percent to have your check cashed. There are vacations on the front porch, where the sun beats down mercilessly on people whose houses are hotter than ovens because they can't afford air-conditioning. There is never enough of anything, so they improvise with extra cups of love, a pinch of humor, and a dash of passion.

My father and Faith showed me one world. Despair and self-hate showed me the other.

healing iv

I said,

"Doctor, I've been holding it in for a long time. I couldn't afford to let myself think about my childhood. A lot of people have had hard childhoods. They don't bring their troubles in to some quack, no offense. What's the matter with me? Why can't I just let well enough be bygones?"

I said,

"Doctor, I just struggle with the straddle. When I'm in polite company, they don't know that I'm not truly a part of them. They bad-mouth the poor. They say that they are poor because they are stupid. They say that nothing good has ever come from the projects. They say that drugs and AIDS are God's retribution for living foul lives. They say that all of us would be better off without the poor, who are like leeches."

I said,

"Doctor, my life is really good now. I don't know why I'm bringing up the past. It's just that things were so bad, and I can't forget. I want to, but I can't find peace. My days are spent running from place to place, trying to do good work and keep myself busy. My nights are haunted by dreams of my mother. She won't let me be. I won't let me be."

I said,

"Doctor, I know people who got hit far worse than I did. Besides, it wasn't often. It really isn't even an issue."

I said,

"Doctor, she locked me in there. There were bugs there. It was dark because the lights were broken. It was like being dead with bugs crawling all around me. Sometimes, I didn't push them off of me. I just let them crawl on me, hoping that they would eat me up, making more and more of me disappear until there was nothing left."

I said,

"Doctor, they called my mother a whore. She gave me my first dose of shame when she lay down with Caramia's dad, who wasn't her husband. She piled on a little more with Freeman's dad, who wasn't her husband. A little more got heaped on with Sojourn's dad, who wasn't her husband. She buried me with my dad, who wasn't her husband. But my father resurrected me. He washed away those other stains, but I still can't get clean."

I said,

"Doctor, they teased me so badly. Sometimes they left me alone, but more often than not, I was game for them. Prey because of something that I had nothing to do with. There were some of them who were darker, too. They were not much lighter than I am. They weren't picked on, though. Why was I?"

I said,

"Doctor, I don't know where I'm supposed to be."

get it together, brother

Freeman lost his job cleaning at the bridge. So he called me.

"Hey, Baby Sis."

"Hi, Freeman. How are you?"

"Good. Look, those crackers fired me."

"Oh yeah? Why?"

"I don't know. Some dumb shit."

That meant that he did something and got caught.

"Oh. What are you going to do?"

"I'll get me another gig, but right now I'm kind low. Could you . . ."

I interrupted him to spare him the shame of having to ask his baby sister for money. But just before

I spoke, I realized that he had no shame. He had never stood on his own, so he had no sense of pride. Without knowing some sense of pride, one can never feel shame.

"How much do you need?"

"I gotta pay my rent."

"How much is rent?"

He told me, and I told him that I would pay it and slide him some money for food and a little for incidentals.

That evening I went to his apartment to drop off the money. When he opened the door, I nervously mumbled something and thrust the money in his hand. I couldn't look into his face, though, because I carried the shame that he couldn't feel.

miss olga's advice

"Listen, child," Miss Olga said, pausing to sneeze while swishing her tea with onions, lemon, honey, and brandy.

"God bless," I said, raising an eyebrow.

"*Gracias*," she returned. "Yes, I called you child. I don't care how old you get. You'll still be my child, whiskers and all."

She rolled her eyes at me in mock sarcasm and settled into her seat.

"I've seen many suns rise and set, and I think I've learned a thing or two. I want to tell these things to you, and I want you to tell them to your niece. She's too young to understand now, but I don't want this to be lost. Call it Olga's *Ocho* Orders, if you want. Just don't lose it.

"Thing one. Know that even in a pile of mush, you can find a kernel of truth. So take that kernel, and remember where you got it. That means listen to everyone. They won't always be learned or lettered, but their voices are valid, so hear them.

"Thing two ties in with thing one. 'Everyone is someone' includes you. Don't you ever let anyone take your heart like you used to let those little girls do. You, Song Byrd, are important, and you serve a purpose. You might not know it yet, but it's true. If you don't love yourself, you'll never love anything that comes from your body. You'll think that your kids are worthless. So love yourself.

"Thing three. Always carry tissues and safety pins.

"Thing four. Know that you are standing on the shoulders of great people. Where you are right now is a progression. All that went on before happened so that you can move forward. So act like it. Don't feel guilty about being successful. Enjoy success. You deserve it.

"Thing five. Always wear clean, neat underwear.

"Thing six. Cuss out one person everyday. Baby, it relieves stress.

"Thing seven. Either go hard or go home. Consistently try your hardest. You'll work up a sweat, and you'll be remembered for being a contender.

"Thing eight. Take a deep breath every day. You'll feel better.

"Here's a bonus. Don't take any wooden nickels. My friend Beetle says that. Now get out. I need to get back in bed. I'm sick, you know."

healing v

He said,

"Song, there's nothing wrong with you. You are completely normal. Yes, a lot of people have had hard childhoods. The strong ones are the people who question it. The strong ones want answers and reasons. Sometimes there are reasons. Other times, there are no reasons that make any sense to us. We have to try to find the ones that we are able to understand."

He said,

"Song, a lot of people are simply out of touch. They are hypocrites. The reason why they are able to live comfortably is because they are underpaying someone else, either directly or indirectly. They live sheltered existences in areas as far away from the poor as possible. And as for AIDS and drugs being retribution, that's just plain old hatefulness."

He said,

"Song, you have to stop running and keep still. That's the only way to hear the answers. Your mother is not haunting you. She is trying to tell you something. She is trying to explain."

He said,

"Song, nobody deserves to be beaten."

He said,

"Song, I can't defend your mother's choices. She thought that she was keeping you safe. I'm sure that if she knew how it would affect you, she wouldn't have done it."

He said,

"Song, you are not responsible for your mother's actions. You can't be held accountable for that."

He said,

"Song, color issues are worldwide. It's not just an American thing. It's not likely to change any time soon. What you can do is explore your skin. Learn it. Know it. Recognize that your dark skin will protect you from diseases that other people will get. Recognize that your dark skin is the color of rich soil from which everything we need grows. Recognize that your dark skin is so beautiful that it's the color that God sees when He closes His eyes. Your skin is rich like Alek's, Roshumba,'s Bethann's, Akosua's Phyllis's, and that pretty old lady who makes my sandwiches at the corner deli. There isn't a wrinkle on her seventy-two-year-old face. The face is like yours."

He said,

"Song, you are exactly where you are supposed to be."

return to the judge's house

Anthony said, "My boy is having a little soiree at his parents' spot, and I told him we'd come. It's not far from your parents' house."

I said, "Cool," and went to the closet to find some "soiree" clothes.

When we pulled in front of the familiar house, dread raced through every part of my body. The Tudor that sat before me looked like a prison, and it held as much appeal. The million-mile walkway was lined with white paper bags in which tea lights flickered. It still wasn't long enough to quell the fluttering in my stomach. Despite the festive-but-sophisticated decorations that adorned the foyer, I felt like I was entering a pen that threatened to hold me until the lions there had surveyed the territory and spotted the weakest lamb.

"Ty," Anthony smiled, greeting someone who looked like he might be the host.

"What's up, Tony? Glad you could make it." He turned to me, looking me up and down.

"Ty, this is my friend Song. Song meet Tyler Marsh, the third."

Summoning up the nerve, I extended my hand, but as much as I protested internally, my grip remained weak and limp as I stood under the gaze of Tyler Marsh, the third. Sensing my weakness, he eyed me even more closely.

"Song. What an interesting name," he commented.

"It serves me well," I returned, trying to meet his cool gray eyes, which swept over me again.

"Well, I'm glad you two could make it. Come on in. The bar is that way, and the food is that way." He pointed toward opposite ends of the house.

"Tyler's my boy," Anthony commented smiling. "I'll go get us some drinks. What would you like?"

"A Kahlua and cream will be fine." I wanted him to stay by my side until I got my bearings, but I'd sound like a kid asking him to do that.

As I stepped further into the house, I was filled with awe. So this is what it's like, I thought. The judge certainly knew how to live. Original artwork lined the peach-colored walls. High-backed, sturdy chairs promised to deliver comfort. An extensive collection of Lladros sat delicately inside of a glass case. Oriental rugs, undoubtedly expensive and authentic, adorned the floor. A portrait of the judge and a woman hung over the fireplace.

As I studied the woman's face, I immediately knew how she had passed his scrutinous eye. Her skin was cream and her curly hair was highlighted with blond streaks. Her full lips were pressed together in what seemed like an effort to make them look thinner. Her blue eyes leapt from the frame. Tyler had inherited her eyes, but she had not passed on the coldness that his eyes held.

"Hey, you," Anthony said, sneaking up behind me.

"Hey," I said turning to face him.

I took the glass from his extended hand, and as I looked at him, the faces in the background solidified in my sight. I felt as if I had been dropped into the vortex of a vanilla cyclone.

"Wow," I said, incredulous.

"What?"

"It's . . . it's a beautiful house."

"Yeah. Tyler's father is a judge, and his mother is a physician."

"Do you know a lot of people here?"

"Yeah. A lot of us went to Central High together. Some went to Princeton with Tyler."

"Oh," I said, wondering if I would be the only chocolate chip in the vanilla spread.

I spotted Sloane across the room talking to her friend Emerson. She smiled and waved, but Emerson drew her attention back to him.

Anthony spent the next half-hour introducing me to his friends, and I spent the evening sinking deeper and deeper into the vanilla cyclone. They inspected me closely, undoubtedly wondering what I was doing there. I wondered the same thing.

There was Wellington, Jocelyn, Samuel, Muffie,

David, Gretchen, Renard, Myles, and Kristi with a K.

"What kind of work do you do?"

"Who are your parents?"

"What do they do?"

"Where did you go to undergrad?"

"Where did your parents go to undergrad?"

"Where do you summer?"

"What clubs are you in?"

"Your hair is so interesting."

I looked around at everyone else's flowing tresses. Some straight, some wavy, curly, but all long. I suddenly felt like I had violated some rule, sneaked in some place that I didn't belong. I excused myself and went to hide in the bathroom. Looking in the mirror, I brushed my hand over my closely cropped hair. I swiped at my eyes as I felt a ball forming in my throat. As I attempted to gulp it back down, I wondered if I would ever fit in.

the robbery

"Chauncey wasn't hurt, but he was pretty shaken up," Anthony said.

"Thank goodness he wasn't hurt."

"Yeah, well, let me go. The cops are here."

"I'll be there in ten minutes."

I focused my attention back on the road. I couldn't believe that the jewelry store had been robbed in broad daylight. Jewelers' Row was one of the safest streets in the city. And Anthony was robbed by another brother.

Rushing into the store, I was unnerved by the sight of police officers around Anthony.

We went to the back of the store to watch the surveillance tape, and I stood next to Anthony as he pushed Play. The camera, which was behind the mirror on the back wall, had a clear shot of the store entrance. On the black-and-white screen, a figure appeared on the other side of the door. Soundless commands were barked at Chauncey as the robber pointed a gun at his head. Chauncey took the cloth sack from the robber and began filling it with bracelets from the nearest display case. As Chauncey made his way down the counter, the robber followed him, gesturing toward some of the jewelry. Chauncey moved to the case closest to where the surveillance camera stood hidden, and he filled it with Rolexes and Movados. The robber, clearly agitated, nervously looked around, and as his face turned toward the camera, I could see his face clearly. Freeman.

in my dream

My mother came to me in my dream last night. It wasn't the first dream that I'd had about her since I killed her, but this dream was so remarkable that I woke up trembling.

She was wearing a red dress as always. I've always associated the color with her blood and her immorality, but not in this dream. In this dream, there were no men hurrying her along. There was no one chasing her with a gun. There were no children weighing her down. In fact, she was floating carelessly along. She was moving upward and upward, and she was holding on to something, but I couldn't see what it was. As she moved upward, she was floating away from me. I was crying and calling out to her, saying, "Mommy, please don't leave me. Mommy, please don't go."

She smiled and reached down for me and she pulled me up to where she was, holding my hand all the while. Then she put me on the other side of her, to the side where she still held something that I couldn't see. She smiled at me, and then she pressed something into my hand. I still couldn't see what it was. When I looked at her again, she was floating away again, but in another direction. I cried for her to wait for me, but she just smiled and pointed to the thing I held in my hand. I looked at it, and I was tempted to let it go because it looked like a regular old string. Then, I figured that if I let it go, my mother would be mad at me. So I examined the string, which seemed to be hanging from something. And when I looked up, I saw a kite the color of water.

the sky

As we drove along the road, cornstalks swished past. It's funny how you look ahead to things, anticipating how they will really look and really feel, but then you get to them, and they speed by in a blur. Then, you struggle to remember how they were.

I struggled to remember my dream from last night because I didn't want it to be a blur. I knew that I had to talk about it or else it would become one. One swishing blur.

"I had a dream about my mother last night."

"Oh yeah. What was it about?" Anthony asked, reaching out to touch my hand.

"She was trying to tell me something."

"Mm-hmm," he commented patiently.

"I've never told you this, but I always thought that my mother hated me."

"How could anybody . . ." he began.

I cut him off. "I was a little girl and I didn't understand that she had had a hard life. She never showed any affection or anything, so I just assumed that I bothered her. Got in her way. I felt like I had stopped her from living. Sometimes when she wanted to go out, and she couldn't afford a baby-sitter, she would lock me in the bathroom so that I couldn't get out and get into something. I would stay in the bathroom for hours just looking up through the skylight in the ceiling. I could only see a little piece of sky, but that little piece gave me hope for some reason. My sister was on drugs, and she needed some money. So I gave her a gun that I had found around the house. It was my mother's gun. Anyway, I gave it to Caramia because I wanted to help her. She looked like she was in so much pain, and I wanted to stop her from hurting. So I gave her my mother's gun to sell. Then, one day, somebody came after my mother. It was the wife of one of my mother's boyfriends. Anyway, she shot my mother, but it was actually me who killed her."

The tears were running hard, and I was tempted to run too. It hurt so much to tell. Anthony pulled over on the side of the road and held my hands while I continued my confession.

"You see, I killed her. I suspected that I always got in her way, but this time, my actions actually killed her. I was in the bathroom when the shot was fired. I could hear the whole thing. I looked up at the sky, screaming and hollering, trying to make the shooting stop, but it didn't. From that day on, I never looked up."

Anthony got out of the car and came around to my side. He pulled me out of the passenger seat while I kept talking.

"But last night in my dream, she took me up there. She gave me a kite that lifted me up into the air, but I didn't want to look up. I couldn't."

My words broke, smothered by the cry gripping my throat.

"Song Byrd. She was trying to tell you to let go of the burden weighing you down. She took you up there because that's where you belong. Let it go."

"I can't. I'm guilty," I sobbed.

"Let it go," he commanded.

I shook my head and buried my face in his chest.

He lifted my chin and turned my face toward the sky. Even with my eyes closed, I could feel the brilliance of the sun, the infinity of the sky. He held my face up, not letting me drop my chin. And then, slowly I peeled my eyes open, and I could see more than a little piece of sky. I could see the whole sky, and its size was magnificent.

epilogue

Our house is filled with the sounds of children. Sometimes the noise is almost deafening, but I don't shush them. Neither does Anthony. We let them play like kids are supposed to.

Our children, Skylar, Paz, Olga, and Felice, love their cousin Maria because she plays with them when she's home from college. She lives with us because Miss Olga's gone. She died last year just as fat and happy as she pleased.

Maria reads stories to the children at night, and they love the tales. But the story they love most of all is the story of Oedipus. They especially love the part when he's reunited with his parents after being lost on a hunting trip on Mount Cithaeron. They ask to hear the story again and again, and I have to remember to keep the lie straight. I remember it, though, and I tell it and smile because everyone loves a happy ending.

azul iii

It's the color of hope.

Azul.

It's the color of a kite.

Azul.

It's the color of the first second that you realize that you are in love.

Azul.

It's the color of your baby's first cry.

Azul.

It's the color behind your lids during your first kiss.

Azul.

It's the color of the first hydrangea blossom.

Azul.

It's the color of the turquoise bracelet that you found in the trash can because someone had discarded it, thinking it worthless. You recovered it, fixed it, and now it's your most precious thing.

Azul.

It's the color of hesitant happiness.

Azul.

It's the color of the ribbon you tie in your baby's hair.

Azul.

It's the color of conservatism.

Azul.

It's the color of true.

Azul.

It's the color from the window of Robben Island.

Azul.

It's the color of a little piece of sky.

Azul.

It's the color of the vast expanse of sky.

Azul.

It's the color of hope.

a little piece of sky

reading group

companion

In deceptively quiet prose, Song Byrd examines some of humanity's most powerful facets: anguish and hope, identity and self-esteem. Her story stirs an urge for dialogue about memories, society, and visions for a wiser future. The questions that follow are designed to enhance your reading group's discussion of *A Little Piece of Sky* and to spotlight particularly insightful passages. We also hope to enrich your personal exploration of this poignant novel.

1. In the first chapter, what does the kite represent to Song's mother? Has its meaning changed when it reappears near the end of the book, in the chapter called "In My Dream?" Why is the kite the color of water?

2. Song spends most of her life believing that she was responsible for her mother's death. As painful as that belief is, does it also help Song cope in some way? Why is it so difficult for her to let go of the notion that she caused her mother's shooting? Why is it significant that Song gave her sister the gun in an attempt to be helpful (thereby gaining Caramia's love)?

3. In "A Happy Day," Song and her neighbor, Miss Olga, delight in simple pleasures such as going to the *mercado* and planting seeds. Was there a Miss Olga in your childhood—a special adult who served as confidante and comforter? Do you fill that role for any young people?

4. Discuss Philadelphia as an ironic choice of residence for Song's mother. Why did she stop running there? Do the novel's characters find liberty or brotherly love in their part of the city?

5. At the height of her career achievements, Song is still haunted by the emotional injuries of her

past. How does this trauma play out in her life? What does it take for her to become more accepting of herself?

6. Like many women in her situation, Song feels ashamed of the very therapy that will help her feel less shameful. She won't even allow any insurance claims to be filed for fear that someone will find out she's seeking help. Why does therapy still carry a stigma for some?

7. Miss Olga's Ocho Orders say a lot about her unique life experiences. Drawing on your past, what pearls of wisdom would you add to the list?

8. How does Linda's story affect Song? What kept Song from falling into a deadly relationship as well?

9. In "Healing IV," Song says, "I just struggle with the straddle," referring to the clash between her poverty-stricken past and the affluent circles she encounters as a fund-raiser. In "Return to the Judge's House," she says that the party made her feel "as if I had just walked into the vortex of a vanilla cyclone." What do these uncomfortable roles say about the definition of "success"? What ef-

fect do they have on Song's self-confidence? Where does Song not feel alienated?

10. Exploring imagery and tone, what transformation do you see from morning to noon, and from noon to night?

11. In spite of her early attempts to change her physical appearance (through hair relaxers that aren't very relaxing , for example), Song manages to maintain a perception of her inner self as beautiful. What keeps that tiny part of herself from succumbing to the sadness around her? Why do you suppose that Nicole Bailey-Williams chose curvature of the spine as one of Song's burdens?

12. In "Mi Padre," Song's father quotes her mother: "I ain't got nothin' left to give. I gave my love. I gave my heart. All I got left is my song." How does this affect your perception of Song's mother at that point? How does that sceene compare to the chapter entitled "My Birth"?

13. The structure of *A Little Piece of Sky* is unusual; brief chapters, all conveyed in first person, alternate between past tense and present. How do these devices affect the storytelling? At any point did you forget that the book is a work of fiction?

14. In "My Inner Self," Song refers to the night sky seen by her ancestors through cracks in the ship that heaved them across the ocean. She too kept her eye on the sky during the terrifying hours she spent locked in the bathroom. In what other ways does Song's life story mirror African-American history?

15. Song's sister and brothers seem less grounded than she is. What are the sources of their pain? How do each of the four siblings stifle their anger? Do you believe that Song's strength is innate, or is it due to the move to her father's house? If he had not accepted her, what might her future have looked like?

16. The novel concludes when Song is finally able to face the sky again, rejoicing in it as if it were an old friend. What did the sky symbolize all those years ago when she vowed to stop looking at it? Is there a little piece of sky in your life?

about the author

© Milton Perry

Nicole Bailey-Williams is a high school English teacher and co-host of "The Literary Review," a book review show which airs on WDAS (1480 AM) in the Philadelphia area. She is also a freelance writer who has penned articles for *Black Issues Book Review, Publishers Weekly*, and *QBR (Quarterly Black Review).* In addition, she was a contributing writer for *Notable Black American Men* (Gale Research) and *Brown Sugar 2: Great One Night Stands* (Simon and Schuster). A graduate of Hampton University, she received a master's degree from Temple University. Mrs. Bailey-Williams was born in Philadelphia and raised in the neighboring suburb of Elkins Park. She currently resides in Mercer County, New Jersey, with her husband, Gregory.